This Book Belongs To:

____

____

____

____

Ant

SPANISH: HORMIGA

PHONETIC: "OR-MEE-GAH"

HOR-MI-GA

- or (like in "or")
- MEE (like in "meet")
- gah (like in "guitar"

ENGLISH

Ants have two stomachs: one for their own food and another one to share food with other ants. They're great at sharing!

SPANISH

Las hormigas tienen dos estómagos: uno para su propia comida y otro para compartir la comida con otras hormigas. ¡Son muy buenas compartiendo!

Bear

SPANISH:
OSO

PHONETIC: "OH-SOH"

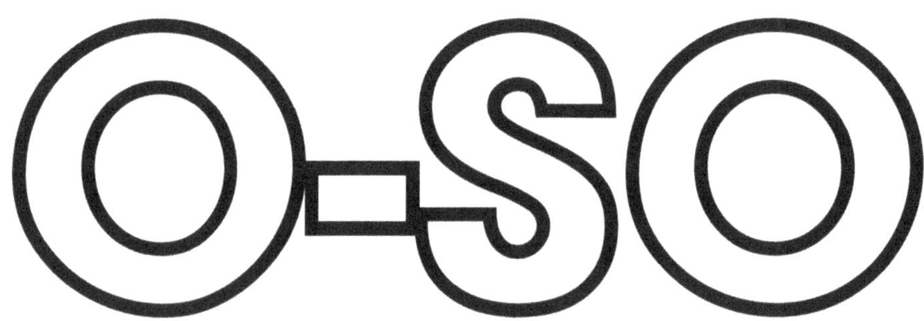

- "OH" like in "go"
- "soh" like in "so"

ENGLISH

Bears have an excellent sense of smell, even better than dogs! They can smell food from miles away.

SPANISH

Los osos tienen un olfato excelente, incluso mejor que el de los perros. Pueden oler la comida a kilómetros de distancia.

Cow

SPANISH:
VACA

PHONETIC: "VAH-KAH"

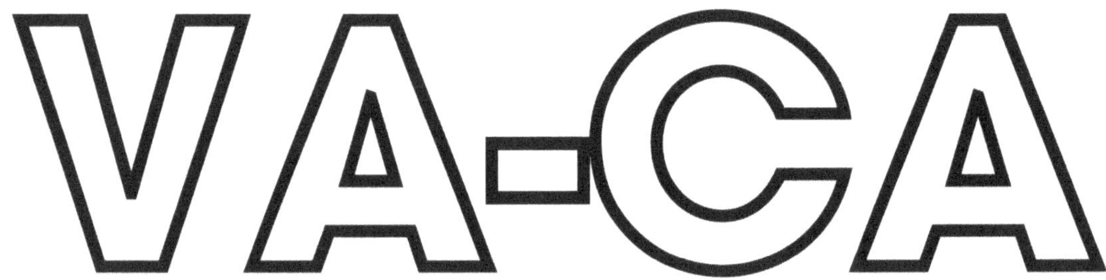

- "VAH" like in "vast"
- "kah" like in "car"

ENGLISH

Cows have a great memory and can remember faces for a long time.

SPANISH

Las vacas tienen una gran memoria y pueden recordar caras durante mucho tiempo.

Deer

SPANISH: VENADO

PHONETIC: "VEH-NAH-DOH"

- "veh" like in "vet"
- "NAH" like in "nah"
- "doh" like in "dough"

ENGLISH

Deer can jump up to 10 feet high and leap as far as 30 feet in a single bound.

SPANISH

Los venados pueden saltar hasta 10 pies de altura y saltar hasta 30 pies de distancia de un solo salto.

Elephant

SPANISH: ELEFANTE

PHONETIC: "EH-LEH-FAHN-TEH"

E-LE-FAN-TE

- "eh" like in "bet"
- "leh" like in "let"
- "FAHN" like in "fawn"

"teh" like in "ten"

ENGLISH

Elephants can use their trunks like a straw to drink water, and they can hold up to 2 gallons at a time.

SPANISH

Los elefantes pueden usar sus trompas como pajita para beber agua, ¡y pueden contener hasta 2 galones a la vez.

Fox

SPANISH: ZORRO

PHONETIC: "SOH-RROH"

- "SOH" like in "so"
- "rroh" like "roll" with a slightly rolled "r" sound

Yak Hair is Waterproof
The outer layer of yak hair is long and coarse, which makes it naturally waterproof. This helps protect them from the cold and wet conditions in the mountains.

La cola del zorro, llamada "cepillo", lo ayuda a mantener el equilibrio y mantenerse caliente en el invierno.

Gorilla

SPANISH: GORILA

PHONETIC: "GO-REE-LAH"

- go (like in "go")
- REE (like in "reel")
- lah (like in "lava")

ENGLISH

A gorilla's arm span is longer than its height, allowing it to swing through trees with ease.

SPANISH

La envergadura de los brazos de un gorila es mayor que su altura, lo que le permite balancearse entre los árboles con facilidad.

Hipo

SPANISH: HIPOPÓTAMO

PHONETIC: "EE-POH-POH-TAH-MOH"

HI-PO-PÓ-TA-MO

- ee (like in "see")
- poh (like in "poet")
- POH (like in "pocket")
- tah (like in "taco")
- moh (like in "mow")

ENGLISH

Hippos are excellent swimmers and can hold their breath underwater for up to 5 minutes.

SPANISH

Los hipopótamos son excelentes nadadores y pueden contener la respiración bajo el agua hasta cinco minutos.

Iguana

SPANISH: IGUANA

PHONETIC: "EE-GWAH-NAH"

I-GUA-NA

- ee (like in "see")
- GWAH (like "gwa" in "iguana")
- nah (like "nah")

ENGLISH

If an iguana loses its tail, it can grow a new one! This is called regeneration.

SPANISH

Si una iguana pierde su cola, ¡puede crecerle una nueva! A esto se le llama regeneración.

Jellyfish

SPANISH: MEDUSA

PHONETIC: "MEH-DOO-SAH"

- meh (like in "met")
- DOO (like in "do")
- sah (like in "salad")

ENGLISH

Jellyfish have been around for over **500** million years, even before dinosaurs

SPANISH

Las medusas han existido durante más de **500** millones de años, incluso antes de los dinosaurios.

Kangaroo

SPANISH: CANGURO

PHONETIC: "KAHN-GOO-ROH"

- kahn (like in "con")
- GOO (like in "goose")
- roh (like in "row")

ENGLISH

Kangaroos can jump really far, up to 30 feet in a single leap

SPANISH

Los canguros pueden saltar muy lejos, hasta 30 pies en un solo salto.

Lion

SPANISH: LEÓN

PHONETIC: "LEH-OWN"

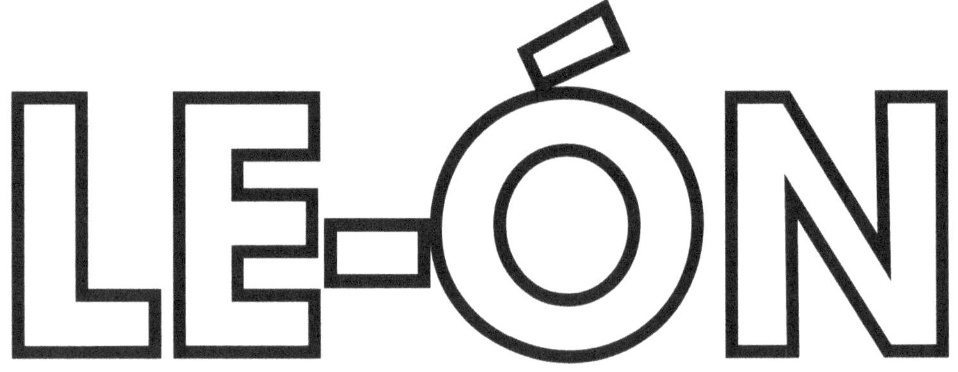

- leh (like in "let")
- OWN (like in "own")

ENGLISH

A lion's roar can be heard up to 5 miles away, making it the loudest roar of any big cat.

SPANISH

El rugido de un león puede escucharse hasta a 5 millas de distancia, lo que lo convierte en el rugido más fuerte de cualquier gran felino.

Mouse

SPANISH: RATÓN

PHONETIC: "RAH-TOWN"

- rah (like in "raw")
- **TOWN (like in "town")**

ENGLISH

Mice can squeeze through openings as small as a pencil because their bodies are so flexible.

SPANISH

Los ratones pueden pasar a través de aberturas tan pequeñas como las de un lápiz porque sus cuerpos son muy flexibles.

Newt

SPANISH:
TRITÓN

PHONETIC: "TREE-TOWN"

- tree (like in "tree")
- TOWN (like in "town")

ENGLISH

Newts can regrow their limbs, tails, eyes, and even parts of their hearts and brains if they get injured.

SPANISH

Los tritones pueden regenerar sus extremidades, colas, ojos e incluso partes de sus corazones y cerebros si se lesionan.

Ostrich

SPANISH: AVESTRUZ

PHONETIC: "AH-VES-TROOS"

A-VES-TRUZ

- ah (like in "father")
- ves (like in "vest")
- TROOS (like in "truce")

ENGLISH

Ostriches have the largest eyes of any land animal, which helps them see predators from far away.

SPANISH

Los avestruces tienen los ojos más grandes de todos los animales terrestres, lo que les ayuda a ver a los depredadores desde lejos.

Pig

SPANISH: CERDO

PHONETIC: "SER-DOH"

- **SER (like in "serve")**
- **doh (like in "dough")**

ENGLISH

Pigs don't sweat much, so they roll in mud to cool off and protect their skin from the sun.

SPANISH

Los cerdos no sudan mucho, así que se revuelcan en el barro para refrescarse y proteger su piel del sol.

Quail

SPANISH: CODORNIZ

PHONETIC: "KOH-DOR-NEES"

- koh (like in "cone")
- dor (like in "door")
- NEES (like in "niece")

ENGLISH

Quails can fly very fast despite being small, sometimes reaching speeds of up to 40 miles per hour.

SPANISH

Las codornices pueden volar muy rápido a pesar de ser pequeñas, alcanzando a veces velocidades de hasta 40 millas por hora.

Rabbit

SPANISH: CONEJO

PHONETIC: "KOH-NEH-HOH

- koh (like in "cone")
- NEH (like in "net")
- hoh (like in "ho")

ENGLISH

Rabbits have teeth that never stop growing, so they need to chew on things to keep them short.

SPANISH

Los conejos tienen dientes que nunca dejan de crecer, por lo que necesitan masticar cosas para mantenerlos cortos.

Snake

SPANISH: SERPIENTE

PHONETIC: "SER-PYEN-TEH"

SER-PIEN-TE

- ser (like in "serve")
- PYEN (like in "pen")
- teh (like in "ten")

ENGLISH

Some snakes can go months without eating because they digest their food very slowly.

SPANISH

Algunas serpientes pueden pasar meses sin comer porque digieren su comida muy lentamente.

Tiger

SPANISH: TIGRE

PHONETIC: "TEE-GREH"

- **TEE (like in "tee")**
- **greh (like in "grey")**

ENGLISH

Tigers can swim very well and often cool off in pools or rivers on hot days.

SPANISH

Los tigres pueden nadar muy bien y a menudo se refrescan en piscinas o ríos en los días calurosos.

Unicorn Fish

SPANISH: PEZ UNICORNIO

PEZ-UNI-COR-NIO

- pehs (like in "pets")
- oo-nee (like "uni" in "unicorn")
- KORN (like "corn")
- yoh (like "yo" in "yoga")

ENGLISH

Unicornfish change colors when they are excited or feel threatened.

SPANISH

Los peces unicornio cambian de color cuando están emocionados o se sienten amenazados.

Vulture

SPANISH: BUITRE

PHONETIC: "BWEE-TREH"

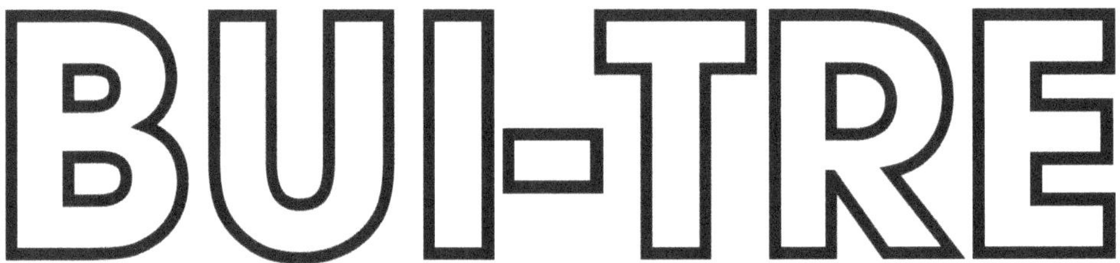

- BWEE (like "wee" in "week")
- treh (like "trey")

ENGLISH

Vultures have a super strong stomach acid that lets them eat things other animals can't, like bones.

SPANISH

Los buitres tienen un ácido estomacal muy fuerte que les permite comer cosas que otros animales no pueden, como huesos.

Wolf

SPANISH:
LOBO

PHONETIC: "LOH-BOH"

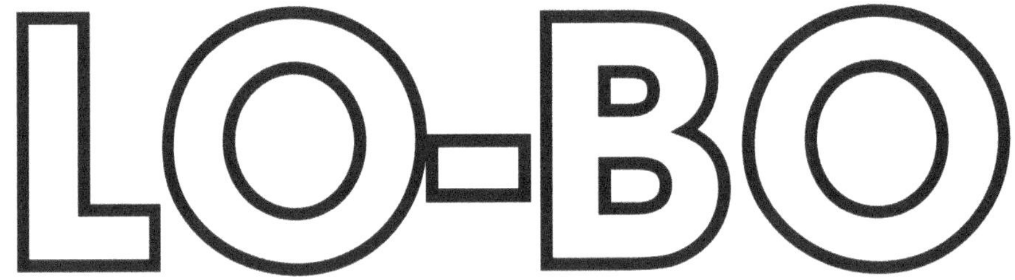

- LOH (like in "low")
- boh (like in "bow")

ENGLISH

A wolf's howl can be heard up to 10 miles away, and it's used to communicate with their pack.

SPANISH

El aullido de un lobo puede escucharse hasta a 10 millas de distancia y se utiliza para comunicarse con su manada.

X-ray fish

SPANISH: PEZ X-RAY

PHONETIC: "PEHS EKS-RAY"

- pehs (like in "pets")
- EKS-ray (like in "X-ray")

ENGLISH

X-ray fish are called that because their bodies are so thin you can see their bones through their skin!

SPANISH

Los peces de rayos X se llaman así porque sus cuerpos son tan delgados que se pueden ver sus huesos a través de su piel.

Yak

SPANISH:
YAK

PHONETIC: "YAHK"

- yahk (like in "yacht")

ENGLISH

A yak's heart is bigger than other animals' hearts, helping them breathe better in high mountains.

SPANISH

El corazón de un yak es más grande que el de otros animales, lo que les ayuda a respirar mejor en las altas montañas.

Zebra

SPANISH: CEBRA

PHONETIC: "SEH-BRAH"

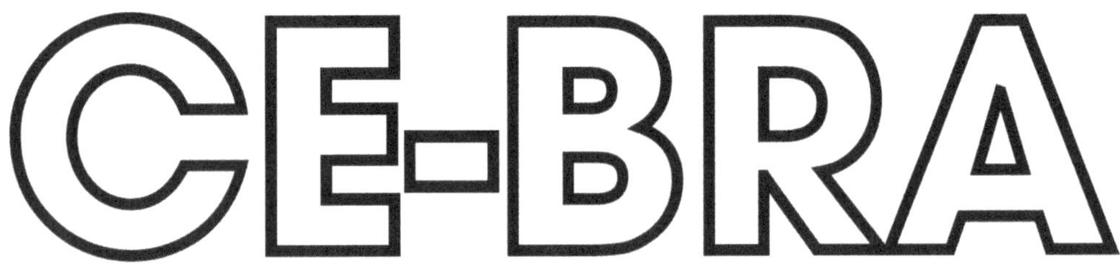

- SEH (like in "set")
- brah (like in "bra")

ENGLISH

Zebras can run up to 65 miles per hour to escape from predators, which is almost as fast as a car!

SPANISH

Las cebras pueden correr hasta 65 millas por hora para escapar de los depredadores, ¡casi tan rápido como un automóvil!